Dandelion Launchers

GW00672212

Reading and Writing Activities
for Units 1-3

PhonicBooks

www.phonicbooks.co.uk   Enquiries@phonicbooks.co.uk
Tel: 07711 963355   Fax: 01666 823 411

Contents

Notes on Dandelion Launchers Workbooks

Dandelion Launchers Workbooks contain a variety of multisensory activities and games linked to the stories in the Dandelion Launchers reading scheme. The activities are designed to help develop the skills underlying fluency in reading and writing.

To become a reader, a learner needs to acquire the skill of pushing together individual sounds to make a word. This process is referred to as 'blending'.

To spell words accurately, a learner needs to be able to break a word up into its component sounds. This process is called 'segmenting'. The learner can then write the letters that represent the sounds in a word.

The activities offered will develop blending and segmenting skills in a fun and accessible way for the younger child.

The workbooks also include activities for letter formation, developing expressive vocabulary through retelling the stories and first comprehension exercises.

Clear instructions for every activity appear at the bottom of each page.

Dandelion Launchers Workbook Units 1-3

Dandelion Launchers Workbook Units 1-3 is divided into three units or levels. Each unit is based on four reading books from the corresponding unit in the reading scheme.

Each unit introduces new sounds but also reinforces those learned previously. In this workbook, the pupil can practise blending and segmenting CVC (consonant/vowel/consonant) words.

Some of the activities in the pack can be done before reading the books and others after reading them. This systematic approach helps the readers to enjoy success at each stage and will motivate them to continue learning.

The sounds introduced in this workbook are:

Unit 1:	s, a, t, i, m	cvc*
Unit 2:	n, o, p	cvc
Unit 3:	b, c, g, h	cvc

* CVC = consonant/vowel/consonant

Planning your lessons

For those who are attempting to teach to read for the first time, here are some suggestions as to how to start, relating them to Unit 1.

1. The lesson should be offered daily, when possible, and not last more than 15 minutes initially with younger children.

2. Introduce the letter sounds for the first unit, one letter sound per lesson. Use the 'Words starting with...' page and the 'Handwriting practice' page for each sound. Use other materials (play dough to make the letters, sand trays to write the letters, alphabet books to identify initial letter sounds). These activities help put the information into memory using the different senses.

3. Once the first three sounds have been learnt, the learner can wordbuild the word 'sat' using the cards on the 'Wordbuilding' page, saying each sound as the word is being built, and then reading the whole word.

4. When all the sounds in the unit have been learnt, the learner is ready to play the games in the back of the four books, as well as the game in the workbook.

5. Always ask the learner to say the sounds and push them together to say the word, when playing a game. The teacher should model this and do the same when playing.

6. You could now introduce the child to capital letters, mentioning when these are used. Encourage the child to find the capital letters learnt in books, magazines etc.

7. Ask the learner to wordbuild the names 'Sam', 'Tam', 'Tim' and the words 'sit', 'sat', 'mat'.

8. The learner should now be ready to read the four books, whilst practising writing skills on the 'Wordbuilding' sheets, and the 'Sentence handwriting' sheets.

9. Once the learner has read a book, ask him/her to retell the story, and to make up other stories.

10. Use the dictation sheets once the children are confident in segmenting words up into sounds and are able to form the letters.

11. The colouring sheets will help reinforce the characters. These will reappear from time to time throughout the books in the series.

Some tips for your lessons

- Lessons should be exciting and fun.

- Give plenty of praise and encouragement.

- Provide small amounts of new learning in each lesson.

- Provide lots of opportunity for rehearsal.

- Make lessons as multisensory as possible, involving the senses of touch, sight and speech.

- Hand success back to the child. If a child reads a word incorrectly, provide them with the missing information so that they can blend the sounds and read the word themselves.

- Use letter sounds, not names.

- Make sure you do not add extra sounds to a sound i.e. 'm' 'a' 't' and not 'muh' 'ah' 'tuh'.

- Encourage the learner to sound out words when reading, writing and playing games.

- Use games as a way to provide needed rehearsal of new learning. Each one of our books has a game at the back which can be photocopied.

Dandelion Launchers

This book belongs to

PhonicBooks

www.phonicbooks.co.uk   Enquiries@phonicbooks.co.uk
Tel: 07711 963355   Fax: 01666 823 411

Dandelion Launchers tick chart
Units 1-3

Unit 1 'Sam, Tam, Tim'

Unit 2 'Pam'

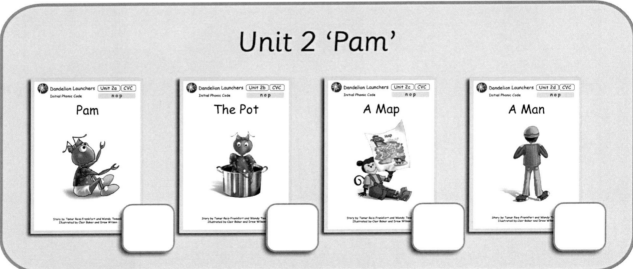

Unit 3 'Bob'

Reading and Writing Activities
Unit 1

Words starting with 's'

Circle the things that begin with the sound 's'.
Draw the letter using different coloured pencils to help with letter formation.
Say the sound of the letter when writing.

(sock, snail, snowman, stamp)

Handwriting practice for the letter 's'

Words starting with 'a'

Circle the things that begin with the sound 'a'.
Draw the letter using different coloured pencils to help with letter formation.
Say the sound of the letter when writing.

(apple, axe, astronaut, ant)

Handwriting practice for the letter 'a'

Words starting with 't'

Circle the things that begin with the sound 't'.
Draw the letter using different coloured pencils to help with letter formation.
Say the sound of the letter when writing.

(teddy, table, tap, tent)

Handwriting practice for the letter 't'

Words starting with 'i'

Circle the things that begin with the sound 'i'.
Draw the letter using different coloured pencils to help with letter formation.
Say the sound of the letter when writing.

(igloo, insect, ink)

Handwriting practice for the letter 'i'

Words starting with 'm'

Circle the things that begin with the sound 'm'.
Draw the letter using different coloured pencils to help with letter formation.
Say the sound of the letter when writing.

(monkey, mouth, mug)

Handwriting practice for the letter 'm'

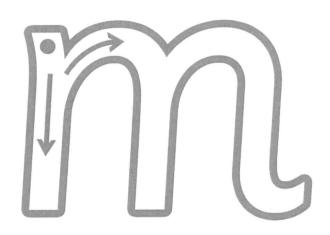

Unit 1 - Sound cards

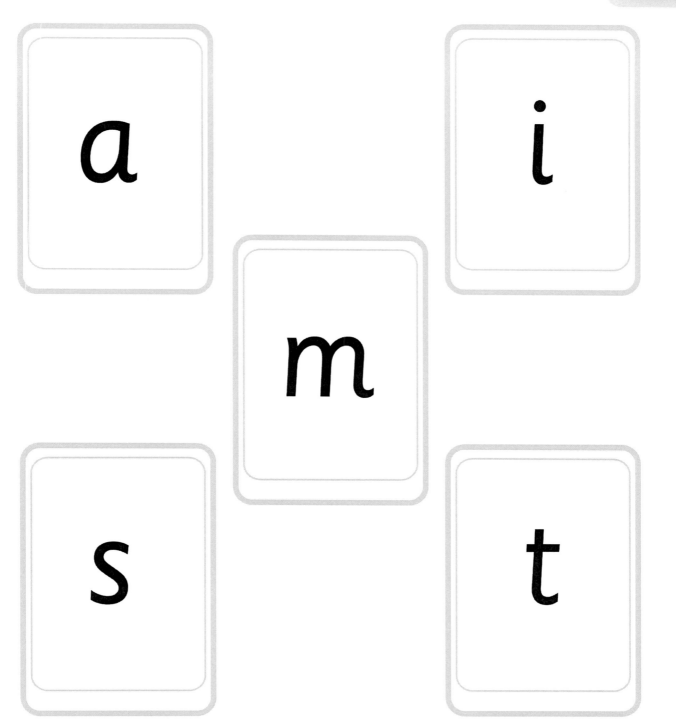

a   m   i

s   t

Photocopy one set of cards per child onto card. They can be used to introduce sounds and for wordbuilding. Photocopy twice to make a simple matching game.

Matching upper to lower case

Cut and paste the cookies to match upper case letters to lower case letters.

Matching lower to upper case

Cut and paste the cookies to match lower case letters to upper case letters.

Wordbuilding cards

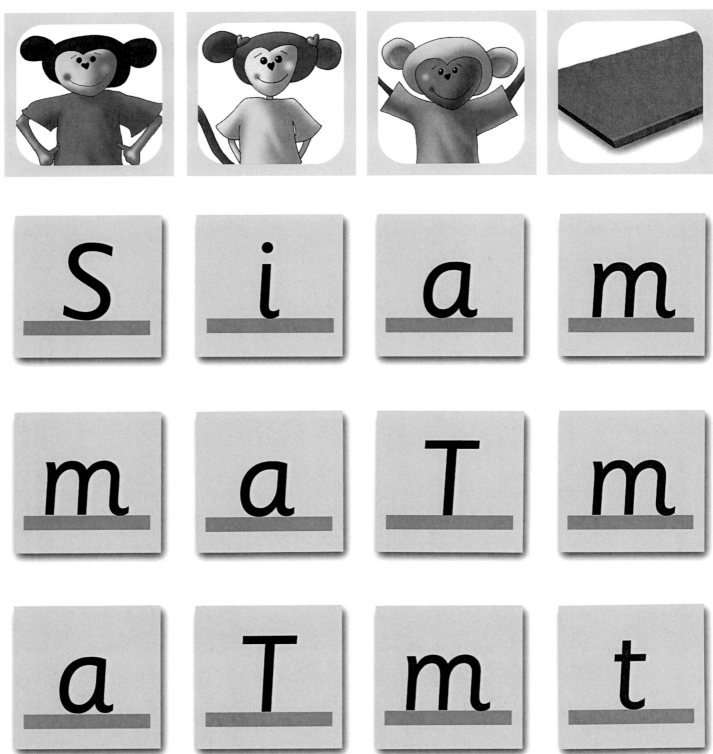

Photocopy this page onto card. Cut out the letters and pictures.
Encourage the child to build the words for the pictures using sounds.
It is important to focus on sounds first, then find the letters that
represent those sounds.

Final missing sound

T a __

T i __

S a __

Fill in the missing sounds. Can be offered as a written activity or using the cut-out squares below.

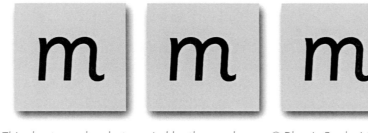

Initial missing sound

___ a m

___ i m

___ a m

Fill in the missing sounds. Can be offered as a written activity or using the cut-out squares below.

T   S   T

Medial missing sound

m ___ t

s ___ m

T ___ m

T ___ m

Fill in the missing sounds. Can be offered as a written activity or using the cut-out squares below.

a a a i

All missing sounds

____ ____ ____

____ ____ ____

____ ____ ____

____ ____ ____

Fill in the missing sounds to make the words. Encourage the child to say
the sounds and blend them together as they write them.

Book 1a - Retell the story

'Sam, Tam, Tim'

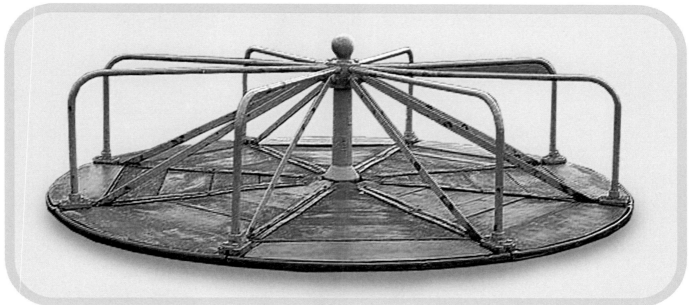

This page can be photocopied onto card. Cut out these pictures for retelling the story or for children to make their own story. Can also be used to reinforce vocabulary.

Book 1b - Retell the story

'I am Sam'

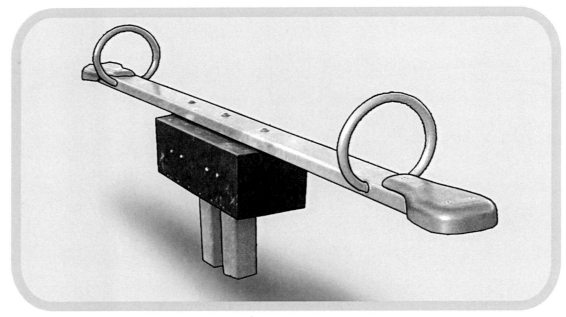

This page can be photocopied onto card. Cut out these pictures for retelling the story or for children to make their own story. Can also be used to reinforce vocabulary.

Book 1c - Retell the story

'Is it Sam?'

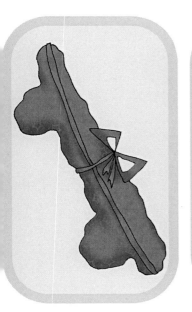

This page can be photocopied onto card. Cut out these pictures for retelling the story or for children to make their own story. Can also be used to reinforce vocabulary.

Book 1d - Retell the story

'On the Mat'

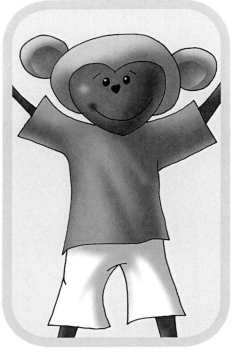

This page can be photocopied onto card. Cut out these pictures for retelling the story or for children to make their own story. Can also be used to reinforce vocabulary.

Word handwriting

am

it

Sam

mat

Handwriting practice for the key words for Books 1a - 1d.

Sentence handwriting

Tam sat.

It is Tam.

I am Tim.

I am Sam.

Handwriting practice for the key words for Books 1a - 1d.

Book 1a - Sentence dictation

I ___ ___ ___ ___ ___ .

Offer the sentence below as dictation. Encourage the children to sound out the words as they spell them.

I am Tim.

Book 1b - Sentence dictation

I _____ _____ _____.

Offer the sentence below as dictation. Encourage the children to sound out the words as they spell them.

I am Sam.

Book 1c - Sentence dictation

I _____ _____ _____ .

Is _____ _____ _____ ?

Offer the sentences below as dictation. Encourage the children to sound out the words as they spell them.

1. I am Tam.

2. Is it Sam?

Book 1d - Sentence dictation

___ ___ ___   is   on

the   ___ ___ ___ .

___ ___ ___   is   on   ___ ___ ___ .

Offer the sentences below as dictation. Encourage the children to sound out the words as they spell them.

1. Sam is on the mat.
2. Tam is on Sam.

Unit 1 - Missing sounds and sentence dictation

___ ___ ___ ___

___ ___ ___ ___

___ ___ ___ , ___ ___ **on** ___ ___ .

Tam, sit on Sam.

This page is intended for revision or for pupils who are moving at a quicker pace and may not need the earlier sheets.

Unit 1 - Comprehension

Sam sat.	I am Tam.
I am Tim.	Sam is on the mat.

Cut out the sentences. Read and match to the correct pictures.

Unit 1 - Sam colouring sheet

Sam

Unit 1 - Tam colouring sheet

Tam

Unit 1 - Tim colouring sheet

Tim

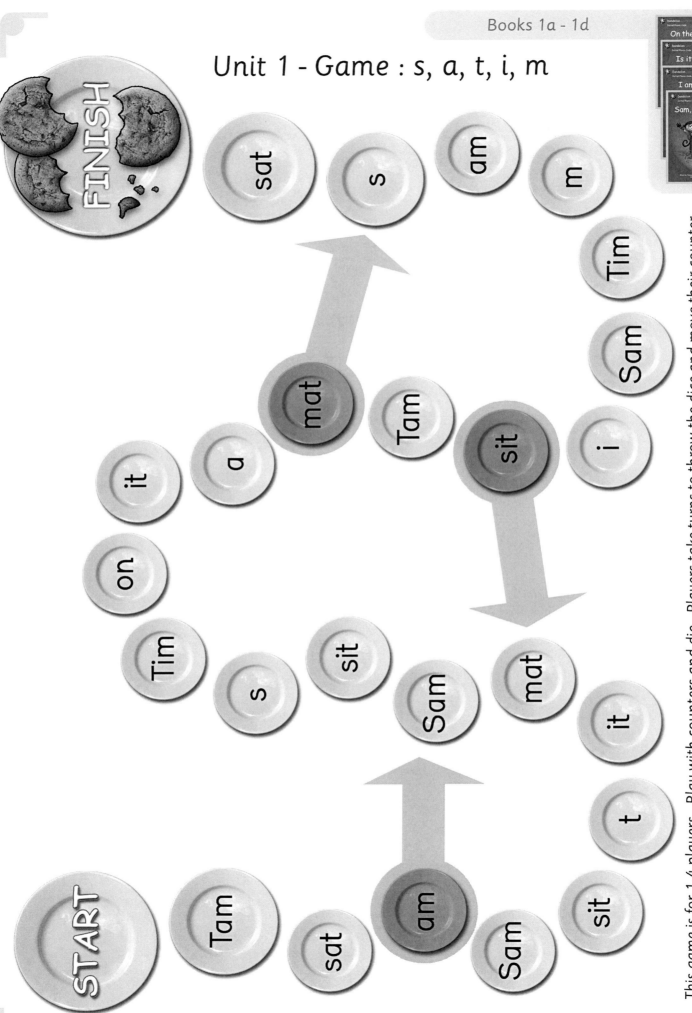

Unit 1 - Game : s, a, t, i, m

This game is for 1-4 players. Play with counters and die. Players take turns to throw the dice and move their counter. Children read the word aloud as they land on it. Make sure the children use sounds rather than letter names.

Reading and Writing Activities

Unit 2

Words starting with 'n'

Circle the things that begin with the sound 'n'.
Draw the letter using different coloured pencils to help with letter formation.
Say the sound of the letter when writing.
(nurse, nest, net, nail)

Handwriting practice for the letter 'n'

Words starting with 'o'

Circle the things that begin with the sound 'o'.
Draw the letter using different coloured pencils to help with letter formation.
Say the sound of the letter when writing.
(orange, off, octopus, ostrich)

Handwriting practice for the letter 'o'

Words starting with 'p'

Circle the things that begin with the sound 'p'.
Draw the letter using different coloured pencils to help with letter formation.
Say the sound of the letter when writing.

(pie, pen, puzzle, pig)

Handwriting practice for the letter 'p'

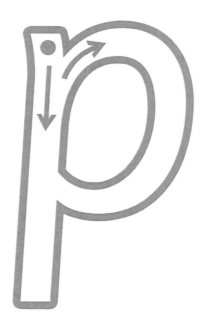

Unit 2 - Sound cards

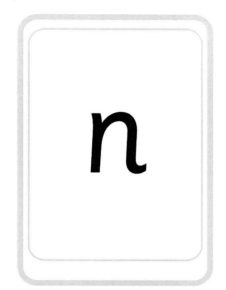

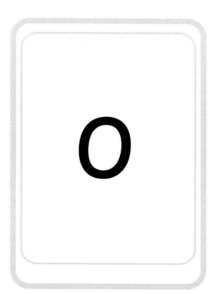

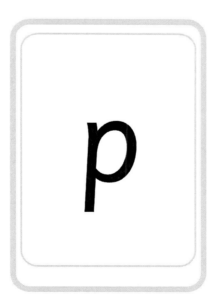

Photocopy one set of cards per child onto card. They can be used to introduce sounds and for wordbuilding. Photocopy twice to make a simple matching game.

Matching upper to lower case

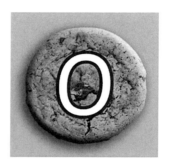

Cut and paste the cookies to match upper case letters to lower case letters.

Matching lower to upper case

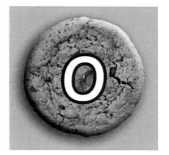

Cut and paste the cookies to match lower case letters to upper case letters.

Wordbuilding cards

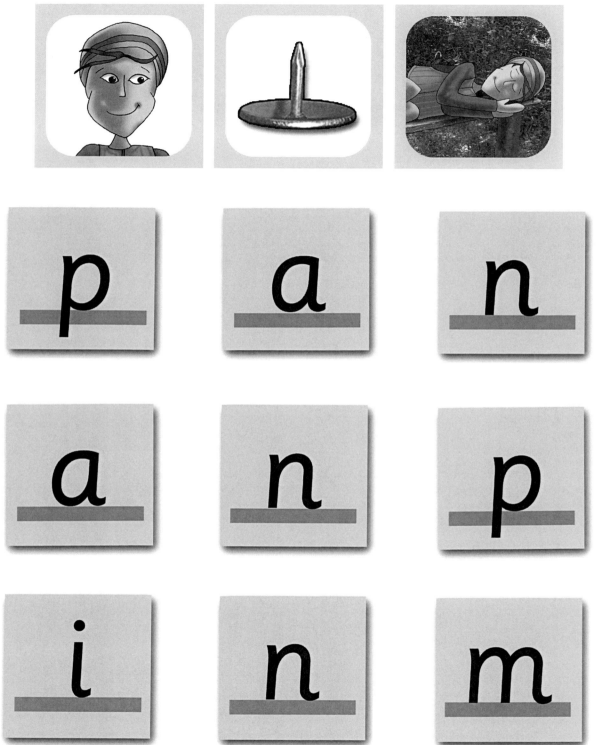

Photocopy this page onto card. Cut out the letters and pictures.
Encourage the child to build the words for the pictures using sounds.
It is important to focus on sounds first, then find the letters that represent those sounds.

Final missing sound

p o ___

P a ___

P i ___

Fill in the missing sounds. Can be offered as a written activity or using the cut-out squares below.

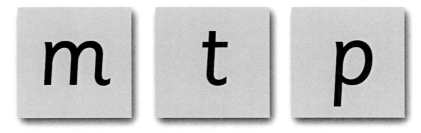

m   t   p

Initial missing sound

_____ o t

_____ a m

_____ i p

_____ a t

Fill in the missing sounds. Can be offered as a written activity or using the cut-out squares below.

  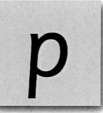 

Medial missing sound

m _ p

t _ n

T _ m

p _ p

Fill in the missing sounds. Can be offered as a written activity or using the cut-out squares below.

 o   a   i   a

All missing sounds

——— ——— ———

——— ——— ———

——— ——— ———

——— ——— ———

——— ——— ———

Fill in the missing sounds to make the words. Encourage the child to say the sounds and blend them together as they write them.

Book 2a - Retell the story

'Pam'

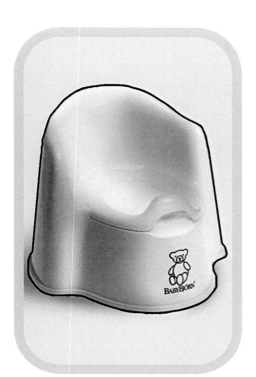

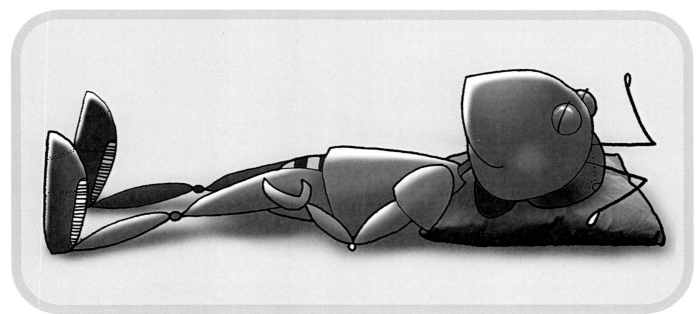

This page can be photocopied onto card. Cut out these pictures for retelling the story or for children to make their own story. Can also be used to reinforce vocabulary.

Book 2b - Retell the story

'The Pot'

This page can be photocopied onto card. Cut out these pictures for retelling the story or for children to make their own story. Can also be used to reinforce vocabulary.

Book 2c - Retelling the story

'A Map'

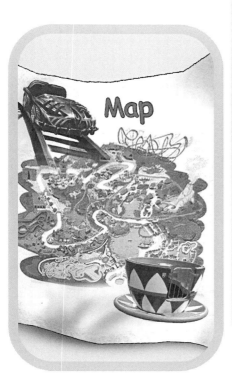

This page can be photocopied onto card. Cut out these pictures for retelling the story or for children to make their own story. Can also be used to reinforce vocabulary.

Book 2d - Retelling the story

'A Man'

This page can be photocopied onto card. Cut out these pictures for retelling the story or for children to make their own story. Can also be used to reinforce vocabulary.

Word handwriting

Handwriting practice for the key words for Books 2a - 2d.

Sentence handwriting

It is Pam.

Not in the pot.

Sam is on top.

Tom is in a pit.

Handwriting practice for the key words for Books 2a - 2d.

Book 2a - Sentence dictation

____ is _____ .

Offer the sentence below as dictation. Encourage the children to sound out the words as they spell them.

It is Pam.

Book 2b - Sentence dictation

I _ _ _ _ _ _ _.

Offer the sentence below as dictation. Encourage the children to sound out the words as they spell them.

I am Pam.

Book 2c - Sentence dictation

hit   the

____ __ ____ ____ .

is

____ ____ ____ .

Offer the sentences below as dictation. Encourage the children to sound out the words as they spell them.

1. Sam hit the tin.

2. Tam is in.

Book 2d - Sentence dictation

____ ____ has a ____ ____.

____ ____ is a ____ ____.

Offer the sentences below as dictation. Encourage the children to sound out the words as they spell them.

1. Tom has a nap.
2. Tom is in a pit.

Unit 2 - Missing sounds and sentence dictation

_ _ _ _ _

_ _ _ _ _

_ _ _ _ _

_ _ _ _ _

_ _ _ _   **is**   _ _ _ _   _ _ _ _ .

Tam is not on top.

This page is intended for revision or for pupils who are moving at a quicker pace and may not need the earlier sheets.

Unit 2 - Comprehension

| Not the pot, Pam. | Pam is on top. |

| The man has a map. | Tam got in. |

Cut out the sentences. Read and match to the correct pictures.

Unit 2 - Pam colouring sheet

Pam

Unit 2 - Pip colouring sheet

Pip

Unit 2 - Man colouring sheet

Man

Unit 2 - Game : n, o, p

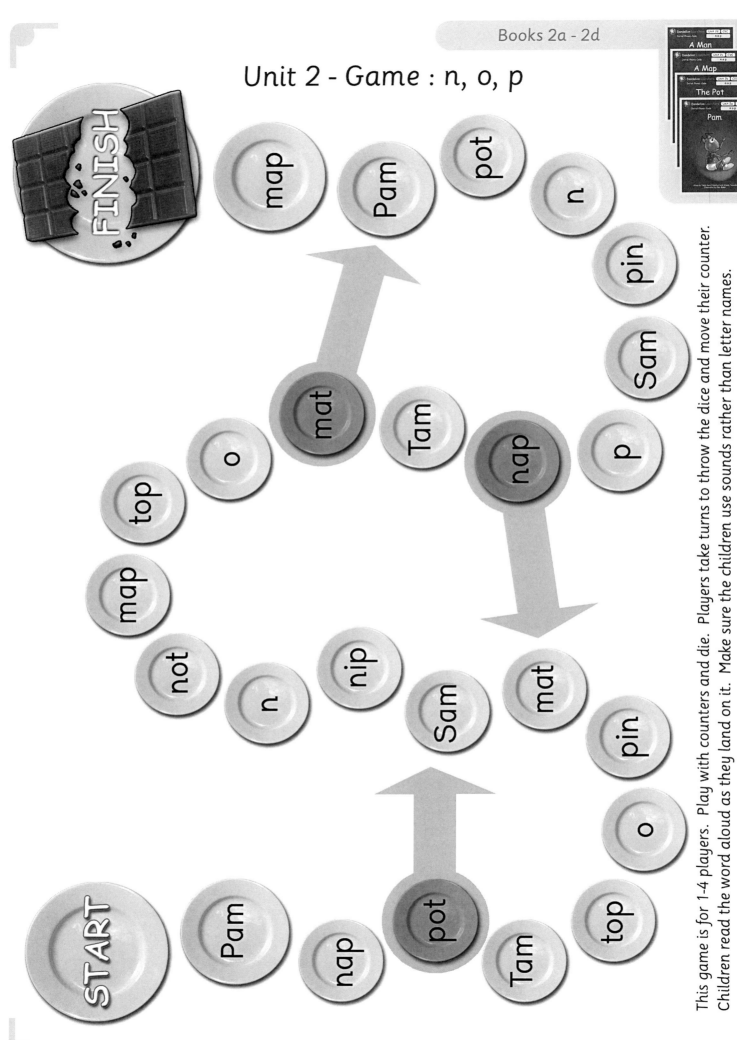

This game is for 1-4 players. Play with counters and die. Players take turns to throw the dice and move their counter. Children read the word aloud as they land on it. Make sure the children use sounds rather than letter names.

Reading and Writing Activities
Unit 3

Words starting with 'b'

Circle the things that begin with the sound 'b'.
Draw the letter using different coloured pencils to help with letter formation.
Say the sound of the letter when writing.

(bike, bag, boat, bath)

Handwriting practice for the letter 'b'

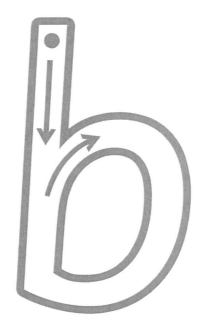

Words starting with 'c'

Circle the things that begin with the sound 'c'.

Draw the letter using different coloured pencils to help with letter formation.

Say the sound of the letter when writing.

(cat, crab, crown, cow)

Handwriting practice for the letter 'c'

Words starting with 'g'

Circle the things that begin with the sound 'g'.
Draw the letter using different coloured pencils to help with letter formation.
Say the sound of the letter when writing.

(girl, goal, gate, grapes)

Handwriting practice for the letter 'g'

Words starting with 'h'

Circle the things that begin with the sound 'h'.
Draw the letter using different coloured pencils to help with letter formation.
Say the sound of the letter when writing.

(handle, horse, hat, hand)

Handwriting practice for the letter 'h'

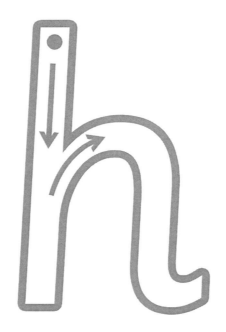

Unit 3 - Sound cards

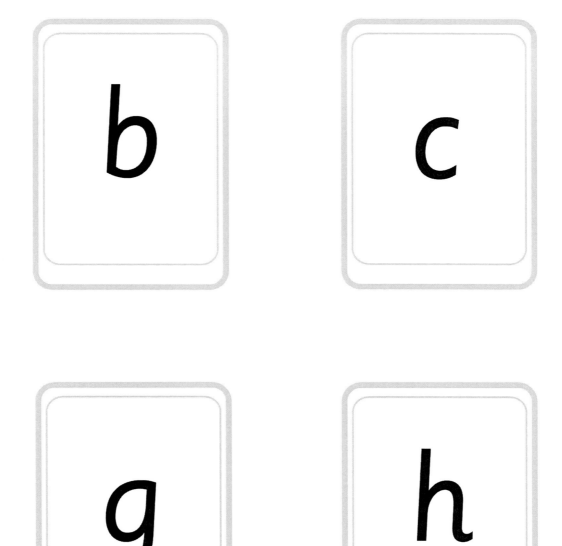

Photocopy one set of cards per child onto card. They can be used to introduce sounds and for wordbuilding. Photocopy twice to make a simple matching game.

Matching upper to lower case

Cut and paste the cookies to match upper case letters to lower case letters.

Matching lower to upper case

Cut and paste the cookies to match lower case letters to upper case letters.

Wordbuilding cards

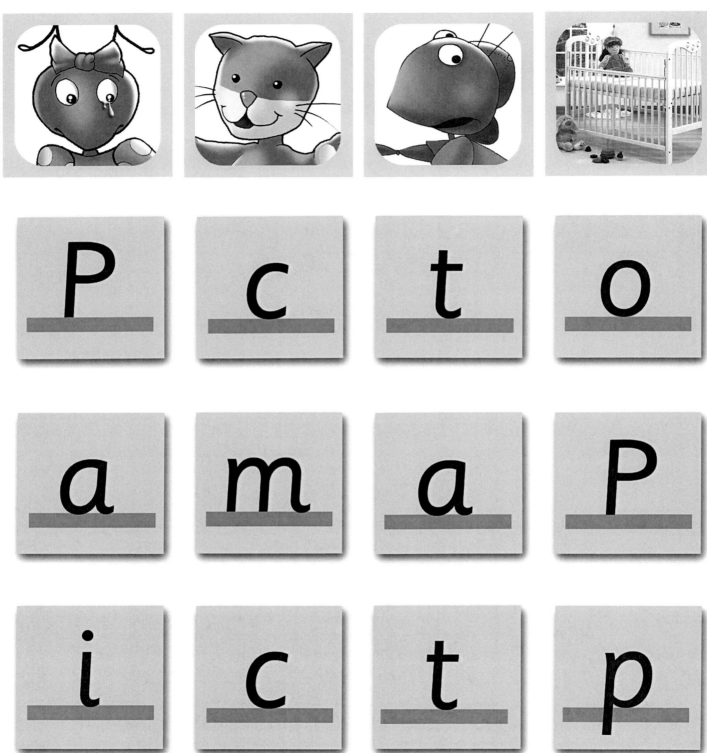

Photocopy this page onto card. Cut out the letters and pictures.
Encourage the child to build the words for the pictures using sounds.
It is important to focus on sounds first, then find the letters that represent those sounds.

Final missing sound

c a __

h a __

c o __

B o __

Fill in the missing sounds. Can be offered as a written activity or using the cut-out squares below.

m   b   t   t

Initial missing sound

_ a p

_ a t

_ a n

_ i p

Fill in the missing sounds. Can be offered as a written activity or using the cut-out squares below.

 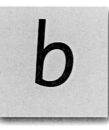

p P c b

Medial missing sound

b __ t

t __ g

T __ m

S __ m

Fill in the missing sounds. Can be offered as a written activity or using the cut-out squares below.

a   a   a   a

All missing sounds

— — —

— — —

— — —

— — —

— — —

Fill in the missing sounds to make the words. Encourage the child to say the sounds and blend them together as they write them.

Book 3a - Retell the story

'Bob'

This page can be photocopied onto card. Cut out these pictures for retelling the story or for children to make their own story. Can also be used to reinforce vocabulary.

Book 3b - Retell the story

'Pip and the Bat'

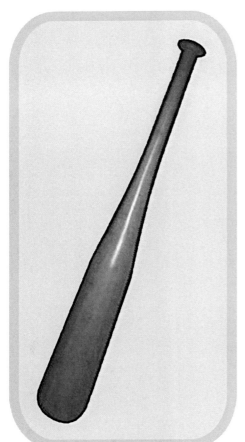  

This page can be photocopied onto card. Cut out these pictures for retelling the story or for children to make their own story. Can also be used to reinforce vocabulary.

Book 3c - Retell the story

'Sam's Bag'

This page can be photocopied onto card. Cut out these pictures for retelling the story or for children to make their own story. Can also be used to reinforce vocabulary.

Book 3d - Retell the story

'Pam and the Cat'

This page can be photocopied onto card. Cut out these pictures for retelling the story or for children to make their own story. Can also be used to reinforce vocabulary.

Word handwriting

Handwriting practice for the key words for Books 3a - 3d.

Sentence handwriting

Bob got the ham.

Pip can hit it.

The bag has a tag.

Cat is in the cot.

Handwriting practice for the key words for Books 3a - 3d.

Book 3a - Sentence dictation

is   a

_____ _____ _____ _____ _____ .

Offer the sentence below as dictation. Encourage the children to sound out the words as they spell them.

Bob is a big cat.

Book 3b - Sentence dictation

__ __ has a __ __ __ .

Offer the sentence below as dictation. Encourage the children to sound out the words as they spell them.

Pip has a cap on.

Book 3c - Sentence dictation

_____ has   a   _____ _____ .

____ is   _____ 's   _____ .

Offer the sentences below as dictation. Encourage the children to sound out the words as they spell them.

1. Sam has a big bag.

2. It is Tam's bag.

Book 3d - Sentence dictation

_ _ _ _ _ _ _ _ _ the _ _ _ _ .

_ _ _ _ has a _ _ _ _ _ _ .

Offer the sentences below as dictation. Encourage the children to sound out the words as they spell them.

1. Pip got the cat.

2. Pam has a big sob.

Unit 3 - Missing sounds and sentence dictation

_ _

_ _

a

_ .

Pip got a big pan.

This page is intended for revision or for pupils who are moving at a quicker pace and may not need the earlier sheets.

Unit 3 - Comprehension

| Pip got a big pan. | The bag has a tag. |

| Bob is a big cat. | Pam sat in the cot. |

Cut out the sentences. Read and match to the correct pictures.

Unit 3 - Sam colouring sheet

Unit 3 - Tam colouring sheet

Tam

Unit 3 - Bob colouring sheet

Bob

Unit 3 - Game : b, c, g, h

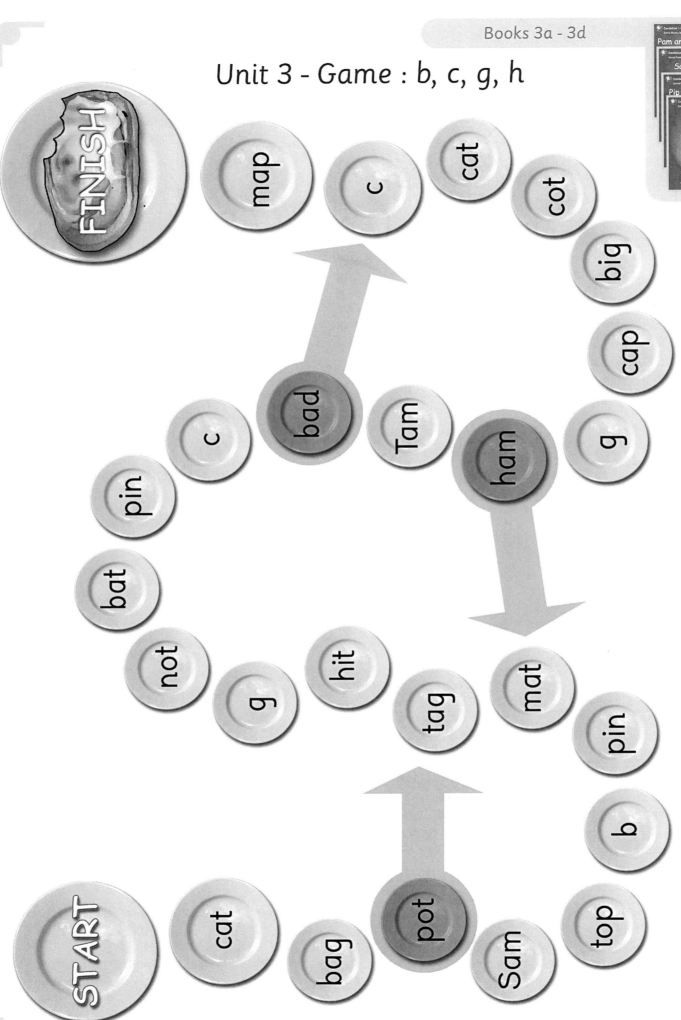

This game is for 1-4 players. Play with counters and die. Players take turns to throw the dice and move their counter. Children read the word aloud as they land on it. Make sure the children use sounds rather than letter names.